November
BOOTS

by Nancy Hundal

 illustrated by Marilyn Mets

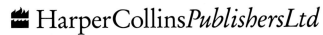 HarperCollins*PublishersLtd*

Produced by Caterpillar Press for
HarperCollins Publishers Ltd
Suite 2900, Hazelton Lanes
55 Avenue Road
Toronto, Canada M5R 3L2

93 94 95 96 97   First Edition   8 7 6 5 4 3 2 1

Canadian Cataloguing in Publication Data
Hundal, Nancy, 1957 -
November boots

ISBN 0-00-223893-4

I. Mets, Marilyn. II. Title.

PS8565.U56N67 1993   jC813'.54   C93-093629-9
PZ7.H863No 1993

Josh's story
— NANCY HUNDAL

For my family
— MARILYN METS

No rain yesterday. No rain today.

I look past the gray window to the sky. The clouds are steel gates, clanged down tight to the earth, locking the sun away until spring. But where is the rain?

Dark window glass throws back a picture of my jacket, mitts and scowling face. And brand new, fire engine-red rain boots.

It's November. The trees shiver. The birds shake. And my red rain boots haven't splashed in a single drop. So where's the rain?

Dad sees my face. "Come on," he says, pulling at my mitten. "Let's find some puddles."

So, puddle hunting, we drive to a playground across town. It is near the sea, in case there are no smaller puddles.

I run to the waterpark. Tall blue and yellow pipes rise from the ground, their spouts cracked and dry. I stomp up and down the cement hills, splashing through a watery memory. But my boots don't remember, so they stay dry.

A leaf flutters past and I chase it to where it drops, into a
mucky pile of yellow, crimson and surprised green.
When I stab the pile with one red toe, the top leaves fly,
light and dry. But beneath they are soggy, like cold porridge.
I see that the rain oozed into the ground yesterday … last week …
before I had my boots.

Dad understands.

"Under the swings, Sir Boot," he says, "there is always a drop or two." We race to the swings, and there is a drop. But not two. I pound that drop with my fire-engine feet until it flees into the ground, cowering.

Then I remember the slide. "There's always muddy muck at the end of the slide, Dad," I call as I run. "Remember last summer, when I went down the slide," as I monkey up the ladder, "and I didn't see the puddle at the bottom until the end and my new runners ..." I stop there because now I also remember Dad's face when he saw my runners.

With a whispery "Whoops!" I push off down the slide. My neck is straining to check for a puddle at the bottom. But just before I hit, I know that there will be no puddle at the end. The puddle was sprinkled down the slide, and now my jeans are stuck to me like yesterday's soggy swimsuit.

I stand at the bottom, seat wet, feet dry. The wind licks at my face with its chilly tongue. Chilly dry tongue. I glare at the sky. Where IS that rain?

My nose, turned skyward, finds smoke trailing by. Someone's burning leaves. My eyes sting and water, water and sting. Water on my pants, in my eyes. Dry boots.

Then another smell hits my nose, doggy-sniffing at the air. A cool finger of breeze from the ocean tickles me under the chin. My boots' water radar leads me to the sea. Dad follows.

At the hill down to the shore, I stop for a moment, then race to the edge. Finally, watery wind pokes into my eyes, around my hood. I love it.

And when my boots hit the little waves — KERSPLOOSH! —they love it too. I pound my feet into the wet sand, and watch the waves creep up to fill in my prints. Then I kick at the bubbly foam, and run back and forth, shouting at the sea gulls. Tiny drops of sea cover my face.

Then one wave rolls higher than the rest, rolls right over my red boots and onto my toes. I turn to look at Dad, and he has seen it too.

"Come on, sport. Time to go!"

So I squish back over the hill, and squelch to the car. All the way home my toes wiggle and squirm in their own little puddles. But still no rain.

Later, I stand with my back to the window, sipping cocoa. My slippers are old, almost worn out, but they know my feet. In the hallway behind me, my boots are dripping and drying.

I hear a tiny tap on the window, something wanting to come in, or maybe just say hello. As I turn, I hear another tap.
And another.

It is the rain, finally come. In the window's reflection, I see a quick red movement, as my boots topple over. I listen to the rain, tapping out its invitation.

For tomorrow.